Oh Brother
Why Is He My Brother??

By **A. Law Shettleworth**
Illustrated By Chad Thompson

Halo ●●●●
Publishing International

ISBN 13: 978-1-61244-329-4
Library of Congress Control Number: 2015900670

Printed in the United States of America

Published by Halo Publishing International
1100 NW Loop 410
Suite 700 - 176
San Antonio, Texas 78213
Toll Free 1-877-705-9647
www.halopublishing.com
www.holapublishing.com
e-mail: contact@halopublishing.com

To my loving husband, Karret Shettleworth, thank you for your love and support.

To Tyrique and Taylen, the joy you both bring your father and me is endless.

A special thanks to my mother, Siu Chun Law.

In loving memory of my father, Thomas Drayton, Jr.

On Sunday morning, Katie was snuggled down in her warm bed when she heard a knock at the door.

She poked her head out of the blankets and yelled, "Who is it?"

"Cockily doodle doo!" her little brother, Richard, shouted. "Katie, it's time to wake up. It's Sunday - pancake day!"

"Go away, Richard!" Katie said.

"Come on, wake up! If not, I'm going to come in," Richard said.

Katie pushed the covers back and sat up. "No! I want you to go away right now or I'll tell Mom!" She waited a moment and then yelled, "Mom!!"

"Well, suit yourself," Richard said. "I'm gonna get pancakes."

Katie heard him run down the stairs. It sounded like a horse; *gallop, gallop and gallop!*

"Urg! He is so annoying," Katie grunted.

She rubbed her eyes, yawned, leaned forward and stretched like a cat. She hopped out of bed and put on her favorite dress. Then she turned around and looked for her bracelet. It was a purple beaded bracelet with M-A-C-Y spelled on it.

She looked left and right. "Ahhhh!" Katie shouted.

Her bedroom door opened and Richard stuck his head in. "What's wrong?"

"I thought you went downstairs."

He shrugged. "I heard you yell, so I came back up."

"I lost my purple bracelet," she said.

Richard pointed. "It's over there under your bed."

"Oh boy, I thought I lost it." She picked it up and smiled. Then she slipped it on her wrist and turned around. "You can leave now."

Richard frowned. "Suit yourself. Your room is boring anyway." He stomped to the door. "And you're welcome!"

SLAM!

Katie heard him stomp all the way down the stairs. "Oh brother, why is he my brother?" she said as she made her bed.

As she started going down the stairs, she saw Richard lying on the floor. "What are you doing down there, Richard? Get up!"

Richard looked up at Katie and giggled. "Why? It's nice and comfy on the carpet."

He started to flap his arms like a bird and roll all over the floor. Katie came down the stairs, and Richard kept rolling on the ground.

"Urg," she grunted. "Richard, you are so dirty. Your white shirt is turning grey!"

"So what? I like grey!" Richard replied.

"Mom, Richard is rolling on the floor again!" Katie shouted.

"Richard, behave now," Mom said. "Or you don't get any pancakes."

"No pancakes! Anything but that!" Richard exclaimed.

As he skipped and hopped along to the kitchen, Katie followed, mumbling to herself. "Why? Why? Oh, why is he my brother?"

Mom prepared colorful treats on the kitchen table. There were strawberries, blueberries, and fresh cut bananas in bowls. And stacks of golden brown pancakes sat on top of each other like space ship saucers.

"Go ahead, wash your hands and stack your pancakes," Mom said.

Katie pushed up her sleeve and turned on the water.

"New bracelet?" Mom asked.

"Yeah, not for me, though, it's for Macy. I promised I would make her a bracelet," Katie replied.

"Such wonderful color! I think she will like it," Mom said.

They all sat by the kitchen table to design their own pancakes. Katie made hers into a smiley face, and Richard made his a mess with dripping syrup.

"What is that, Richard?" Katie asked. "You have syrup everywhere!"

"The Amazon! All I need is a few blueberries in the syrupy river then it's done."

Katie rolled her eyes. "What? That looks like a big mess!"

They both reached out to the bowl of blueberries at the same time.

"Hey, I got it first," Richard shouted.

"No, I did and give it to me!" Katie said.

"There are enough blueberries for you both," Mom said.

16

But they went back and forth, and *CLICK, CLOK, CLING*! The bowl dropped to the ground. Blueberries rolled all over the kitchen floor.

Katie folded her arms. "Look what you did, Richard!"

"You started it!" Richard cried.

Mom stood. "You are both to blame. Now, let's get this cleaned up."

They rushed to pick up every single blueberry.

"Ahhhh!" Katie shouted.

"What's wrong now?" Richard asked.

"I lost my purple bracelet again," she cried.

Richard pointed. "It's over there under your chair."

Katie grabbed the bracelet and found that something else was missing. "My bracelet is missing a bead, the letter Y. Oh no, what am I going to do now? Macy is going to be so mad at me."

She started to cry.

"Don't cry, Katie. Macy is not going to be mad at you," Mom said.

"But I promised I would give her this bracelet, and she will be here at noon."

"Don't worry, I'll help you find it," Richard said. "I'm good at finding stuff."

He crawled under the table while Katie looked under the plates.

"Ah ha!" Richard cheered. "It's right here."

"Where?" Katie asked.

"Here." He lifted the bowl of blueberries. "The letter Y is right here mixed with the blueberries!"

They both laughed.

Mom clapped her hands. "There, everything is fine now."

Katie took the letter Y bead and put it back on the bracelet.

She smiled at Richard.

"What?" Richard said.

Katie gave him a big hug. She whispered into his ear, "You are the best brother in the world."

"Aw, let me go. You're squishing me," Richard said.

Katie laughed. "Come on. Let's go make some more pancakes!"

CPSIA information can be obtained at www.ICGtesting.com
Printed in the USA
BVIW12n0024270215
389004BV00005B/16